A Century of Charades

William Bellamy

Contents

PREFACE. 7
I 7
II 8
III 8
IV 9
VI 10
VII 10
VIII 11
IX 11
X 11
XI 12
XII 12
XIII 12
XIV 13
XV 13
XVI 13
XVII 14
XVIII 15
XIX 15
XX 15
XXI 16
XXII 16
XXIII 17
XXIV 17
XXV 17
XXVI 18
XXVII 18
XXVIII 18
XXIX 18
XXX 19
XXXI 19
XXXII 20
XXXIII 20
XXXIV 20
XXXV 21
XXXVI 21
XXXVII 21
XXXVIII 22
XXXIX 22
XL 23
XLI 23
XLII 23
XLIII 24
XLIV 24
XLV 24
XLVI 25
XLIII 25
XLVIII 25
XLIX 25
L 26
LI 26

LII.. 27
LIII... 27
LIV... 28
LV 28
LVI... 28
LVII.. 28
LVII.. 29
LIX... 29
LX... 29
LXI... 30
LXII.. 30
LXIII... 31
LXIV 31
LXV.. 31
LXVI... 32
LXVII.. 32
LXVIII... 32
LXIX... 32
LXX 33
LXXI... 33
LXXII.. 33
LXXIII... 34
LXXIV... 34
LXXV 34
LXXVI... 35
LXXVII.. 35
LXXVIII... 35
LXXIX... 35
LXXX 36
LXXXI... 36
LXXXII.. 37
LXXXIII... 37
LXXXIV... 38
LXXXV 38
LXXXVI... 38
LXXXVII.. 39
LXXXVIII... 39
LXXXIX... 39
XC 40
XCI... 40
XCII.. 41
XCIII... 41
XCIV... 42
XCV.. 42
XCVI... 42
XCVII.. 43
XCVIII... 43
XCIX 45
C.. 46
KEY TO ANSWERS... 48

A CENTURY OF CHARADES

BY

William Bellamy

PREFACE.

To give an answer to a riddle is like explaining a joke,—something never to be done, unless reluctantly, and with averted face, as Strato held the sword for Brutus to fall upon. But as we all like to be told when we are right, and as the first answer that suggests itself may not be the one that fits best, I have prepared a key by which any guess may be confirmed if correct or rejected if wrong. The mathematical mind that is better at exhausting combinations than at catching allusions may use it as a last resort to obtain a solution. To start fair let me state that my charades are all accurate either to the sound or to the spelling, but not necessarily to both, and that the parts into which my words are divided are all monosyllables.

W.B.

DORCHESTER, MASS., October, 1894.

I

MY first endured a hundred years,
A prodigy of logic and of wit;
My last the faro banker fears,
King Solomon was not arrayed like it.
My whole, dear reader, you'll divine
When you peruse this book of mine.

II

MY first, offender 'gainst agrarian laws,
Was shot, for no one would defend his cause.

On Mansfield Mountain once did dwell
A youth who did my second well.

In gaudy hues my whole you see
A-cheapening a pound of tea.

III

'T is pleasant in these shortened days
To sit before the chimney's blaze,
And hear afar the stirring sound
Of hunter's horn and baying hound.
When pussy, for he loves the heat,
Stalks in to claim his favorite seat,
I drop the paper half unread,
To scratch poor pussy's head instead;
And think how vain are business cares,
How vain the strife of bulls and bears.

Without, I catch my second's din,
I listen to my first within,
And learn from both the lessons blent
Of healthy sport and home content.
If stocks should rise, I would not sell;
If stocks were down, I'd fare as well :
That very kettle seems to sing

That riches are not everything.
I think I'll ask my broker, though,
If consols are my whole, or no.

IV

MY first will measure less than four feet long,
'T was often fifty in Quintilian's day;
My second is the fertile source of song,
The sweet bird's carol, not the poet's lay.
My third in hills is apt to congregate;
A worker, though addicted to the bowl
In Massachusetts, but in New York State
She's frequently a lady, and my whole.

V

THERE'S something very queer about
The girl I love and seek to win;
I wish that I could find her out,
Perhaps I have been taken in.

To doubt the lady were a sin,
Sincerely though, I've come to doubt
She ever meant to let me in,
Because I always find her out.

I asked to be allowed to call,
And modestly she gave consent;
Now servants tell me in the hall
She's not my first, she came and went.

Inconstant as the scented gale
That from my second idly blows,

Elusive as a phantom pale,
I only know she comes and goes.

Though hope may counsel still my third,
Eternal hope that smiles at dawn,
My heart is sick with hope deferred
To hear again she's been and gone.

I'd seek her at the frozen pole,
Chimeras fight and Gorgons rout,
I'd brave the fire of my whole,
If she were in and not put out.

VI

MY first bedeck the lawn
When the moon is shining bright;
My second ends the dawn,
Beginning every night;
My third and fourth is done
To hide a thing from sight;
My whole's the name of one
Whom we can't remember quite.

VII

NO longer for the Roman dame
My second from my first is brought;
Where once the Roman legions fought
No terror has the Roman name;
My whole is master of the soil,
And reaps in peace the fruits of toil.

VIII

A PRODUCT of coniferous trees,
A hardy toiler of the seas;
These make when joined and matched,
A Russian scratched.

I make this statement wholly on
The authority of Napoleon.

IX

I SOUGHT my first in starry skies
Where shines the April sun;
My second came before my eyes,
And warned me to be done.

'T is very hard to lose one's sight;
I 'm blind as bat or mole;
Once hills and fields were my delight,
Now I 'm no more my whole.

X

MY first is high,
My second damp,
My whole a tie,
A writer's cramp.

XI

THE student, from the Charles returning,
Upholds my first, the seat of learning.
My last disturbs the baby's sleep;
My whole's a monster of the deep.

XII

JUST round the corner of the street
Your roving eyes my first will meet;
I think you know the little square,
And recognize a number there.

The sage of Athens wisely said,
"Count no man blest until he's dead."
Behold Lesseps, his nation's pride,
With honors heaped on every side,
Does Honor on his age attend ?
Alas ! my second is his end.

The wretch who long has sought in vain
Relief from torturing fangs of pain,
No more my whole with horror sees,
But hails ' short pang that brings long ease.'

XIII

MY first is found where Glory leads,
The coward fears and fools despise;
In common walks my next precedes,

It aids the fallen wretch to rise.
My third was once a robber count,
His castle stood the Rhine beside;
My whole some ladies learn to mount,
But no one ever cares to ride.

XIV

WHEN to my second men confide
My third that they have hoarded,
It is my first, and if they bide
My whole will be rewarded.

XV

MY first bends graceful by a spring;
My last has conquered many a king;
My whole to gales and frost and snow
Of Winter adds another woe.

XVI

MY first, a heathen god of old,
Was fashioned in a mighty mould;
My whole on him was brawny, vast,
He swung a hammer, or my last.
His worshipers have passed away;
Like every dog he had his day;
He and his kin have met their fate,
And Odin's halls are desolate.
Ask not his name, nor vainly seek;
He's knocked into the middle of next week.

XVII

THOU manikin that fain wouldst ape
Of human form the godlike shape,
Fetish sure from Ashantee!
Raising beauteous arms to thee,
Maids repeat a fervent prayer
That winds may lull and skies be fair.

Thy dual parts let me proclaim;
The first the earliest fruit of shame,
The second, worn, decrepit, bent,
Was woman's guard and ornament,
Or haply, foremost of the ten,
Stood up to be assailed of men.

High perched above, thou dost bestride
Thy narrow throne in pygmy pride;
Snowy bosoms heaving high
Palpitate beneath thine eye,
Womankind for offering bring
All to which they closest cling.

What Beauty's touch has sanctified,
What Modesty would seek to hide,
What binds the mother to her child,
In sacrifice to thee are piled;
And the blushing virgin's zone
Is loosed for thee, and thee alone.

XVIII

BENEATH the ground
My first is found.

My last two wear
A cross of hair.

And my complete
Is very sweet.

XIX

WHEN Death came to my first, he still delayed
To smite the fairest flower his fields could show;
And so the lady lingered, and they said,
"When the leaves fall." Before she sank too low
They brought her pigeon to my next. She tried
To smile her thanks while toying with the bird.
The doctors held a council ere she died,
And spoke faint-hoping, fearing to my third.
At last the end came. As the hours dragged slow,
She pressed my whole, and said with feeble moan,
"Farewell, my treasure, whither I must go,
I go without thee : Time is there unknown."

XX

WHEN young Lochinvar had come out of the west,
To appear at a wedding he hardly was dressed;
His heart might be bold and his steed might be fast,

But he must have been wet after swimming my last;
And a bridesmaiden whispered, "I call it a shame,
One would think that he had n't my first to his name.
Does he not look my whole? What a horrible mess!
They are going to dance! She will ruin her dress!"

Yet he was no slouch, for it must be confessed
In a very few moments his suit he had pressed.

XXI

O CHILD of Sorrow! born to feel
The tread of Penury's iron heel,
To wander friendless and alone,
To ask for bread and get a stone;
Two things thou lackest, which possessed,
Riches were thine, and life were blessed.
But name them in a whispered breath;
To speak them dooms a king to death!

XXII

MY first the anxious mother often hears;
My second is the vaunted cup that cheers;
When coming through my third, two bodies met;
Before you ride, my fourth you have to get.

You'll guess my whole if you will think a bit;
It is a sort of touchstone for your wit.

XXIII

MY first has led a blameless life,
He never quarrels with his wife,
His inmost thoughts are free from sin,
He's happy when the tide is in,
He never seeks my whole to raise,
His taste is worthy of all praise.
Yet such existence who would wish to live
Long as my last presents alternative?

XXIV

WHERE flows my first, bright burning,
My second marks a shoal;
The fisherman, returning,
Espies it with my whole.

XXV

THERE are two plants yon often meet,
And one is bitter, one is sweet;
Conjoined, two different words they make
According to which first you take:
One compound is a lofty state,
The other has fallen much of late;
A lack of one the Indian counts a gain,
Blood of the other soils the arms of Spain;
Divide the one, and Anna's name appears,
The other's bark keeps ringing in my ears.

XXVI

UPON my first I've often sat;
My second is a kind of hat;
My whole, a sort of creeping thing
That Noah from the ark did bring.

XXVII

OF course it is not literally true
To say my first the king can never do;
Many a deed of English kings I've heard
Might well be styled my second and my third;
But in the sense in which it is intended
The saying's true until my whole is ended.

XXVIII

I HIRED Pat to drive a pig;
The price he asked I thought was big.
"Bedad," said Pat, "you don't suppose
I'll lade the craycher by the nose;
Perhaps your honor'll tell me how
Convaniently to drive a sow:
Before she's in my first my second,
My whole a pittance you'll have reckoned."

XXIX

THE reindeer fattens on my first,

My second would disdain it;
An army marched full many a verst
To take my whole with gun and bay'net.

XXX

MY FIRST

I AM a worm with fiery head,
My venom serves to wake the dead.

MY SECOND

Upon the ocean's verge I stand,
A seamark for a rugged land.

MY WHOLE

When Nature lay in silent sleep,
And Darkness brooded on the deep,
Before the morning stars had sung,
Or ever seraph's harp was strung,
Ere Brahma wakened from his dream,
Or Indra was, I reigned supreme.

XXXI

IF milk be added to my first,
You have an antidote for thirst.

A blade of grass my second, or
A weapon to attack a boar.

My whole was held for many a year
The prince of poets without peer;
Now comes a reputation-knifer
To make him out the merest cypher.
Unless I'm very much mistaken,
He can't succeed, to save his bacon.

XXXII

To make my last upon my first,
The poet's lyre oft is struck;
My whole, with fire-water cursed,
Loses his head and runs amuck.

XXXIII

To make my first, a lamb will serve
If one fore-quarter we reserve.

My next is good to speed a bolt;
Don't ever feed it to your colt.

My last through Henry's visor broke;
Montgomery dealt the fatal stroke.

Since Mercy rides in Horror's van,
Hail in my whole man's love to man!

XXXIV

ALTHOUGH it was a base my whole,

The umpire cried, "My first at first."
The player who to second stole,
A second in my second cursed,
Then turned upon his heel about:
No wonder that he was pat out.

XXXV

O MAIDEN, with your lips apart!
You know my first, and feel its smart.

My last, the path of dalliance, leads
'Twixt hedges sweet to flowery meads.

We call my whole a man of prayer;
What need of farther praise is there?

XXXVI

QUEEN MARY on the scaffold stood,
My second with my first she viewed.
Despite her crimes we mourn her doom,
And twine my whole upon her tomb.

XXXVII

I LOVE my whole, men always will
While men are men and might is right;
'T is more than courage, more than skill;
In man or beast it gives delight.
We hear the thunders rumble yet
That Webster from the rostrum hurled;

(It was my first, but men forget
The customs of the ancient world.)
The land still echoes with his fame,
A glamour clings about his name;
Just take away my last, and see
How singular his words would be.

XXXVIII

MY first might tempt an anchorite,
A symphony in pink and white.

The days of pagan Rome are past,
When slaves were offered to my last.

A village all unknown to fame,
My whole is linked to Shakespeare's name.

XXXIX

THROUGH Syrian desert rode my first,
Oppressed with heat, o'ercome by thirst:
My second was his quest.
More proud was he on helm to bear
The token of his lady fair
Than red-cross on his breast.

My whole for lady fair is known,
Her cheek is red, her heart is stone,
A fatal beauty aye!
And those who feast upon her charms
Rush to their death with open arms,

With open eyes they die.

XL

WHEN he who changed my first in vain
Dragged in my whole great Hector slain,
He vowed that dogs and crows should rend
The slayer of his dearest friend;
But when old Friam sued to pay
The rites were due that bleeding clay,
The hero, melting at a father's woe,
Showed for my last what he denied his foe.

XLI

I SHIPPED aboard the Betsy Jane;
My first was fresh and fair;
We manned my whole and hove the chain;
The mate stood by to swear:
To hear him take God's name in vain
Would raise a lubber's hair.

She stepped aboard the Betsy Jane;
My last was fresh and fair;
We kissed, and hoped to meet again;
A rose was in her hair.
I kissed my sweetheart once again;
The mate forgot to swear.

XLII

MY first is two, my second more;

My whole brings many to death's door.

XLIII

ALAS! no more beneath the winking stars
My lover carols at my window bars;
My cruel father came with angry toe;
Not even my first would he have treated so.

I'd fly to him, but whither could we go?
I'd drown myself, but duty whispers low;
On some fond breast the bleeding heart relies;
Oh, if my second could but sympathize!

Ah! what avail the precepts of the wise?
I hate my whole, which never satisfies;
My spirit batters 'gainst its prison bars,
And scorns the thorny pathway to the stars.

XLIV

MY first gives promise of a fruitful year,
My second in the fountain plays,
My whole the statesman's art displays,
And gets the vote of every British peer.

XLV

MY first pours out at early teas,
My last is anything you please,
My whole's the cause of much disease.

XLVI

IF you are hungry as a bear,
And love the hermit's simple fare,
My second in my first prepare;
That't is my whole, you will declare.

XLIII

THE milkman my first at my second is leaving;
He vows that he loves me, but men are deceiving;
Yet where is the maid would believe he could lie
When my whole can be read in his honest brown eye?

XLVIII

YE dudes who make your dress your care,
And dance attendance on the fair,
Answer this question if you can,—
Does worth or habit make the man?
But for my whole this counsel take,
That clothing oft my first will make.
By women would you be admired?
Then in my last be well attired.

XLIX

MY hair is falling down my first,
I'm sure I must a perfect fright be,
I think my corset lace has burst,

Oh, how I wish my third I might be!
For if my whole could work the spell,
Or some kind-hearted wizard hear me,
I'd take my second in a shell,
I'd play baseball and none would jeer me.
Without my skirts, how queer't would seem;
No mouse would fright, no tramp appall me;
'T would be just lovely as a dream,
And all the girls my fourth would call me.

L

HAPPY the man whose dreams by night
No cares disturb, no fears affright,
Whose conscience pats him on the head,
And puts him in God's arms to bed.
Unlike him Scotland's guilty queen
Who walked in sleep with hand unclean:
Not all the waters of my first
Could wash away the spot accursed;
Not all the water in my whole
Could cleanse my second from her soul.

LI

'T WAS bitter cold, the sky was gray,
And night was falling fast,
When, as I took my homeward way,
I chanced upon my last.

I lifted up the little waif,
My first, and almost dead;

Beneath my cloak I clasped it safe;
"'T will please my whole," I said.

And I remembered as I went
The text in the New Testament,
How sparrows have a Father's care,
Another whole is every hair.

LII

FAST through my last our vessel sails,
All snug aloft, the topsails set,
Sou'westers glistening in the wet,
The combings flying o'er the rails.

It lifts a little on our lee,
Rings out the lookout's warning shout,
Sharp comes the order, "Put about."
How near my first appears to be!

'T was there the Dreadnaught left her bones;
I hear the seabird's plaintive dirge,
And loud the breakers and the surge
Repeat my whole in dismal tones.

LIII

EXPLAIN this riddle if you can:
A bird and beast once made a man;
That man begat a numerous race
Devoid of every Christian grace.
It makes me shudder in my shoes;

His children in their blood he brews!

LIV

MY first is headgear of Ismail;
My last rebukes the lazy sinner;
Hang up my total by the tail,
And when it falls, ask me to dinner.

LV

SAY not my first your guessing power transcends,
You have it almost at your fingers' ends;
Nor for my second Russian realms explore,
Since you can find it at your very door;
And one, the leader of a wandering band,
Can beat my whole with time-defying hand.

LVI

MY first applauds an actress nice,
My second catches men and mice,
My whole is just a cheap device.

LVII

MY first commends both wine and wit,
But books and bottles not a bit.

A handy tool my last, but those
Who wield it must look out for toes.

I wandered in the forest glen,
And wished my whole were back again.

LVII

MY first was once a king uncouth,
The lord of subterranean fires;
And, if its people told the truth,
My second was the land of liars.

Undoing by night the labor of each day,
Ulysses' queen her suitors kept at bay.
A pattern wife, as husbands all agree,
She was my whole, if wife my whole can be.

LIX

FROM tennis courts my first ascends;
My second in commotion ends.
No martyr's crown my whole secured,
Who worse than martyrdom endured;
They found who tore his limbs apart
A lady's image at his heart.

LX

THE WIDOWER'S WOOING

I HASTENED to my lady's side,
For Cupid through her lashes beckoned;
I longed to clasp her as my bride;

I asked her : Would she be my second?

She frowned, but when I heaved a sigh,
Her frown relaxed, her lips she pursed;
We kissed, though she protested I
Behaved unseemly to my first.

We sat together and I sought
To show how soul communes with soul;
But she was teacher, I was taught,
And found in her my perfect whole.

LXI

WITHOUT me women would become my first;
(Won without wooing how could they be dear?)
My second, if the storm in fury burst,
Makes each red flash a redder flash appear,
The wind's sad moan a sadder moan to hear.
My whole, presented oft to childhood's view,
Less frequent seen as each succeeding year
Illusions vanished make emotions few,
Is still to Youth or Age a wonder ever new.

LXII

WITH all his imperfections on his head,
My second to my first untimely fled;
My whole a lady hight who scorned to wed;
Of both in Shakespeare you have surely read.

LXIII

HAD I my first, not with my first I'd toil,
Nor with my second burn the midnight oil;
I'd choose a book, my whole that book would be,
And give the day to laughter, mirth, and glee.

LXIV

THE traveler's solace in the dusty heat,
Castlereagh's likeness, joy of them that thirst,
The sinking sailor's hope,—behold my first!
Which merry dancers trample under feet.

My second comes when sons and fathers meet
Brothers and sisters on one bosom nursed;
Old age laments its loss, of all the worst,
And heaven without it seems but incomplete.

Within my hollowed whole, in humid cell,
An erring wife was by her lord confined;
The rest is silence: he who kept her well
Could soul enthrall as well as body bind;
And now the startled rustic often spies
From out her prison glare two ghostly eyes.

LXV

MY first preserved my last, and every spring,
To deck each comrade's grave my whole shall bring.

LXVI

WHETHER my first exists, men disagree;
My second never was and ne'er shall be.
'T was in my whole a highland lassie's ear
Caught the faint sound that told of succor near.

LXVII

DESTROYERS both, but different in way;
This, sharp and sudden; that one, timely, kindly;
These make my whole, a giant in his day,
Who prayed for light, and, maddened, perished blindly.

LXVIII

BLAME not the lover that he pleads;
If stars our lives control,
Blame not the maiden that she cedes,
And softly lisps my whole.

Ah, fatal word and oft accursed!
Let him no man be reckoned
Who from a maid could take my first
Before they had my second.

LXIX

To spell a word of six,
Two letters might suffice;

That word defines the rest,
It makes a virtue vice.
Those letters two, reversed,
Reveal his name who laid
His head upon the block,
By woman false betrayed.

LXX

HIS battles fought, aside were laid
The sword and armor of the knight;
My last has dulled his trenchant blade,
My first has dimmed his corselet bright.

And he, that knight of noble soul,
Whose hand was open, heart was great;
His life is clouded by my whole
His love, corroded into hate.

LXXI

THE stars are out, my whole has ceased,
And silence reigns in earth and sky,
Save for my first, that yelping beast,
My second hate him more than I.

LXXII

THE ripple of my first is heard
Where 'neath my second I conferred
With seven kings, and made my third.

LXXIII

IN times of universal greed,
One scarce knows when to give or heed
My first, which leads the lamb astray,
Or bodes disaster to the bay.

My last has privilege always
Upon his sovereign to gaze:
A right as old as ancient Sparta,
As full confirmed as Magna Charta.

Full oft in street or public square,
My whole goes whizzing through the air;
While housewife trembles for her window-pane,
And panting boy leaps after it in vain.

LXXIV

MY first from oat a mountain came,
My last like origin may claim,
Of one of Shakespeare's plays my whole 'B the name.

LXXV

MY first was in a temple kept,
And listened while its guardian slept.

My second was the word he gave
Who died the bravest of the brave.

My whole, men risk their lives to reap,
Betwixt the mountain and the deep.

LXXVI

THE maiden with her fortune in her face
My first repeated with an artless grace.

'T was in my second Julius Cæsar fell;
'T is in my second Worth can still excel.

The temperate man, contented with enough,
Avoids my whole, he deems it perilous stuff.

LXXVII

MY first is curious to relate,
My last is stupid, obstinate;
My whole the first King Richard wore,
'T was worn by Cromwell long before.

LXXVIII

MY first is true, so is my next,—
So true that none deny it;
My whole, it is a question vexed
If bride should make or bay it,

LXXIX

MY first is such a stupid dunce

He never uttered sense but once.

My second gazed with bated breath
At Bayard on his bed of death.

Fair in my third my total grows,
A panacea for life's woes.

LXXX

MY first mid Roman thousands stood,
And each was to each other peer;
My next is iron, sand, or wood,
And Patti sang it loud and clear;
When God to Adam spake my third,
The earth was his to till and ear:
My whole, may nevermore that word
Upon our statutes reappear
To blot our commerce from the seas,
And palsy honest Labor's hand;
Our flag should float to every breeze,
Our trade be free with every land.

LXXXI

BRINGING sweet pain and glad unrest,
My first has pierced a maiden's breast,
Shot straight from Cupid's bow;
Persuade her not my second's naught,
Be sure her heart is better taught;
She 'll shame you with her "Oh!"

And I am wealthy, fat, and fair;
My golden locks demand my care;
I sail the ocean wide;
That little maiden waits for me;
And when my ship comes in from sea,
I 'll take her for my bride.

LXXXII

UNDER my first the chief was laid,
His warring spirit could not rest;
Oft for his grace his lady prayed
To Mary, mother ever blest.

But one wild night when all was dark,
When gibbets creaked and no cock crew,
The lady raised her head to hark;
My second must be his, she knew.

His hot breath told from whence he came;
She went with him without a word;
As ready she to share his flame
As Scævola to brave my third.

Pity the dead who pass unshriven;
O Mary, mother, rest each soul!
To love like hers is much forgiven,
He died for Scotland on my whole.

LXXXIII

MY first once made the Romans fear,

My last falls soft on lady's ear,
My whole delights to chase the deer.

LXXXIV

MY first, a sacred river,
Flows to a sunless sea;
My next was doomed forever
To be followed by a bee;
My third I do that you can guess my whole,
Which Cadmus out of Egypt stole.

LXXXV

I WATCHED the riders show their skill;
And some rode well, and some rode ill;
It was my whole who rode the worst,
Although he quickly passed my first.

But when he strove to pass them all,
'T was fit that pride should have a fall;
And since the accident occurred,
He's on my second and my third.

LXXXVI

MY first was not a plumber, but a god;
His pipes are laid and he himself is dead.
My next has been wherever man has trod,
And oft, fantastic, turns a woman's head.
Let others for Golconda's treasures pine,
My third would suit me better if 't were mine,

My whole shall in the blessed season come,
Speech to the deaf and language to the dumb.

LXXXVII

YOUNG Harry was a love-sick swain,
He wooed a maiden fancy-free;
Full long he sighed, and sighed in vain;
She teased him with my one, two, three.

At last she chose to ease his pain,
And now she's kind as kind can be;
So I may build my nest again,
These happy days were named for me.

LXXXVIII

A CITY'S scourge, a toper's cheer,
My first is to the ladies dear;
Though in the harem held in fear.

Denied to many a wedded pair,
My second is as free as air;
The just and unjust have their share.

Once England was my whole, before
The Norman landed on her shore,
And Harold weltered in his gore.

LXXXIX

A FISHERMAN renowned for lies

Boasts of a famous cast;
When on my first he lands his prize,
He finds it is my last.

His friends the tale with laughter greet,
And mirth beyond control;
His words they vow that he shall eat,
And ask him to my whole.

XC

LULLED by my deadly first, a beauty slept.
My second is the seer that o'er her wept.
Doubtless her captor was to anger stirred;
If so, he was my second and my third.

Where shall my whole contrive to dwell,
Which Britons from their homes expel,
Exclude from heaven, and deny to hell?

XCI

OF Don Hnidizo el Timyd,
Who fell on Zama's fatal plain,
The deeds of arms might shame the Cid,
And put to blush the flower of Spain.
My first informs yon what he did:
Alas! it all was done in vain.

His dame besought his vassals' dole,
And raised my second for my whole.

XCII

MY first is just a cad,—I trust yon know
What that is, I do not; he is one, though.
My last was called ridiculous, but why?
Perhaps he 's no more so than you or I;
He 's got that name, however, and 't will stick.
My whole was once a dentist, I suppose,
Who "Teeth Implanted," but a story grows
In telling. As the Spaniards say, who knows?
For now the legend is, he sowed them, thick.

XCIII

MY first relieves a lover's woes;
It comes unbidden, like the wind it goes.

Though a Jew's riches are my last,
No Jew will keep it, yet he holds it fast.

The solemn stars that view serene
Man's joy and sorrow, shame and pride,
The oyster, fattening 'neath the tide
Of Narragansett's waters green,
The country churchyard's grassy knoll,
And he who spake not overmuch,
But rescued Holland for the Dutch,
Though different each, are all my whole.

XCIV

STITCH, stitch, stitch!
In poverty, hunger, and thirst,
A woman toils though her fingers itch,
Striving to finish my first.

Break, break, break!
With chisel, and jimmy, and blast,
A man works on, though his fingers ache,
Striving to shatter my last.

Drink, drink, drink!
The poison that seethes in the bowl;
My heart is sad whenever I think
Of the murder wrought by my whole.

XCV

MY last is two pipes, and my first is one;
My whole has many a maid undone.

XCVI

MY first once formed a state
Where Plenty smiled and Commerce sate.
My second is the guinea's stamp,
And Caesar had it in his camp.
When on a wall my third is spied,
The prudent pass on t'other side.

My whole in old Maynooth
Begged in the market-place;
His word was simple truth,
His was a hopeless case.

XCVII

MY last says, "Seamen all, beware
My first, or you 'll be stranded there."

My whole might be, if I but chose,
A beauty pert with flashy clothes,
A figure trim, a ready wit,
A pretty foot with shoe to fit.

But otherwise I choose to make her:
In colors sober as a Quaker,
Dull, cold, and dumb, no sign of waist,
Lack lustre eyes, with nose effaced,
And no one could admire her feet,
Yet all her lovers think her sweet.

XCVIII

MY first the Hindu priest repeats;
The fakir in Benares streets,
Standing with withered arm in air,
Has made of it a constant prayer,
Expecting by his abnegations
To skip a crore of transmigrations;
He thinks he knows the shortest cut
To 'scape from Being's endless rut.

A merry life led Robin Hood
In Nottingham and green Sherwood;
He liked to feast on haunch of buck,
And tip the can with Friar Tuck.
Perhaps you 've heard an old ship-master
Spin yarn of peril and disaster
Where, in a time of danger great,
My next was Tuck's associate.

My third can easily be found,
'T is often heard and always round;
The child is early taught to know
It centres in each joy and woe;
Although it nothing well expresses,
It makes most dignified addresses;
If you and I were hand and glove,
This go-between might cool your love.

Can there be men of level pate
Believe the stars prognosticate?
Who in the Bible run a pin
Ere enterprises they begin?
I hold such things but idle fancy,
Like gypsies' cards and chiromancy;
Much better oracle my last!
It tells the future, present, past.

A pompous man, erect and tall,
Had come to make a formal call;
His solemn tones, his mien sedate,
His portly form, his air of state,
His look at once severe and mild,

Made great impression on a child,
Who sought her ma with cheeks aflame;
The mother asked the caller's name;
The child returned this answer odd:
"I don't know, but I think it's God."
She deemed him, little simple soul,
The incarnation of my whole.

XCIX

OLD Sol pursues his annual track
Around the time-worn zodiac;
Calls back the robin and the crow,
The swallow and the bird of snow,
The ulster and the palm-leaf fan,
The oyster- and the lobster-man,
The sleigh-bell's chime, the locust's hum,
The crocus, and chrysanthemum.
Of all the months he yearly brings,
To fly on golden or on leaden wings,
Let memory my first recall,
The shortest, sweetest of them all.

Gladys, you fill me with surprise;
You tell me that you botanize!
It only seems the other day
My love for butter you 'd essay,
That dandelion heads you blew
To see if mother wanted you,
And pulled the daisy's leaves apart
Without a flutter at your heart.
Now you examine with a lens
The exogens and endogens;

Perhaps my second you have tried,
And found it with the bark inside.

Some love the sunny wine of Spain,
And some the cru of Aquitaine,
Others grow mellow on hard cider,
And others merry with dry Schreider,
A few may sing the praise of hock,
While millions love their Grerman bock,
The gourmet sips his red Burgundy,
Old maids drink tea with Mrs. Grundy;
No honest preference I assail,
From "forty-rod " to "Adam's ale;"
But when I quaff the flowing bowl,
My favorite tipple is my whole.

C

WHEN Israel was about to die,
He bade his sons come hear him prophesy.
Ranged round his bed, he called them each by name,
And each received his words of praise or blame;
The treacherous water, and the men of wrath,
The lion's whelp, the serpent in" the path,
The hind, the haven, and the fruitful vine, The bounteous table spread for
kings to dine, The overcomer of the men of brass,
The ravening wolf, the doubly-burdened ass.

My second is an ass also,
That, 'twixt my first and third, two curses, couches low.

'T is said the Prophet, journeying in the heat,
Beheld my whole resplendent at his feet;

His ravished eyes surveyed its rivers twain,
Tracing their verdant ribbons on the plain,
Its marble baths, inviting to repose,
Its groves of orange, and its bowers of rose,
Its market-places piled with luscious food,
Its rich bazars that teemed with every good,
Its mart for slaves, where stood his heart's desire
Whose kiss were peace, whose bosom cooling fire.
Full long he viewed the panorama spread,
Reluctantly he turned his horse's head,
And pitched his tent amid the desert's dust.

For great is Allah, Allah's ways are just;
Much though he give, he much to man denies,
And not to man his ways he justifies:
One paradise is his decree;
Who taketh this on earth foregoes the one to be.

KEY TO ANSWERS.

NOTE.—This key is not intended to divulge the answers, but to verify the correctness of a guess. Substitute for each letter of a supposed answer the figure standing over it in the table. If the number thus formed is the one given in the key, your answer is correct.

1	2	3	4	5
A	B	C	D	E
F	G	H	I	J
K	L	M	N	O
P	Q.	R	S	T
U	V	W	X	Y

KEY.

1—3 3 1 3 1 4 5
2—3 3 3 5 3 5
3—1 1 3 3 3 1 4 5
4—5 2 5 2 1 4 5
6—4 4 1 1 4 5 3 5
6—4 1 4 5 4 2 1 3 5
7—1 1 3 3 5 3
8—5 1 3 5 1 3
9—3 1 3 2 2 5 3
10—3 5 1 3 5 4
11—4 3 1 2 1 4 4
12—1 5 3 3 5 1 4
13—1 3 5 5 5 2 3 1 1 3

14—4 4 4 1 4 5 3 5
15—1 13 4 1 3 5
16—5 3 5 3 1 4
17—3 2 5 5 3 5 4 1 4 4
18—3 5 2 1 4 4 5 4
19—3 5 1 5 1 5 5 3
20—2 3 5 5 5 4 2 1 5
21—3 3 5 3 1 3 1 5 5
22—3 3 4 5 5 3 4 5 4
23—3 2 1 3 5 3
24—4 5 2 4 2 3 5
25—3 1 1 5 6 1 5 3 1
26—3 5 1 5 4 2 5
27—4 5 4 1 4 5 5
28—4 5 4 1 5 4 4
29—3 5 4 3 5 3
30—4 6 4 2 2 4 6 4 4
31—4 3 1 1 5 4 1 5 1 3 5
32—3 1 2 1 5
33—1 3 2 1 2 1 4 3 5
34—5 15 3 1 2 5
35—3 3 1 1 2 1 4 4
36—4 3 4 2 1 4
37—1 3 5 3 5 4 4
38—3 1 3 2 5 5
39—4 4 2 3 5 4 3 1 4 5
40—2 1 3 2 1 2 5
41—3 4 4 4 2 1 4 4
42—5 1 3 5 3
43—4 5 2 3 1
44—2 1 4 2 5 5
46—5 5 5 5 3 4 4 2
46—4 1 1 5 3 2

47—3 1 4 4 6 3
48—2 1 4 4 1 4 3 5
49—4 5 3 3 5 3 1 4 3 5 3
50—2 1 4 4 4
51—3 3 4 2 4 3 5 4 4 1 3 2 5 3 5 4
52—3 5 1 3 1 4 4
53—5 1 3 5 2
54—1 3 5 1 4 1 4 5 6 6
55—2 1 4 3 1 4 5 5 1
56—3 2 1 1 5 3 1 1
57—4 3 5 1 4 4
58—4 4 4 3 3 5 5 5
59—2 5 2 4 5 6 3
60—1 4 6 3 8 4 4 6
61—3 5 4 4 5 8
62—4 4 4 4 1 4 4
63—1 4 3 1 3 4 3 1
64—1 1 3 1 1 4 4
65—2 1 3 2 1 4 4
66—2 1 3 1 4 5 3
67—1 5 1 4
68—1 4 4 3 5 5
69—5 4 3 5 4 4
70—3 4 4 5 3 1 4 5
71—3 1 3 1 5 3
72—1 5 5 5 4 5 1 5 5
73—5 4 1 3 1 5
74—3 5 1 4 5 5 3 1 1
75—4 1 3 1 3 4 3 5
76—4 1 3 1 5 4 5
77—3 1 4 3 1 4 4
78—5 3 5 1 4 4 5 1 1
79—1 4 1 3 5 4 5 2

80—5 3 2 1 3 2 5
81—4 3 116 6
82—2 1 4 4 5 3 1 2
83—3 1 4 5 3 5 4 4
84—1 2 1 3 1 2 5 5
85—2 4 3 5 3 2 4 4
86—1 1 4 5 5 3 4 3
87—3 1 2 3 5 5 4
88—4 1 4 5 4
89—2 1 4 2 1 5 5
90—1 4 1 4 3 1 6 5
91—3 1 4 4 5 3
92—3 1 4 3 1 4
93—4 4 2 5 4 5
94—3 5 3 2 5 3 1
95—2 1 5 5 5 4
96—3 5 4 4 4 3 1 4
97—2 1 3 2 5 2
98—5 3 4 4 1 5 6 5
99—3 5 4 6 8
100—4 1 8 1 4 8 1 4

The Codes Of Hammurabi And Moses
W. W. Davies

QTY

The discovery of the Hammurabi Code is one of the greatest achievements of archaeology, and is of paramount interest, not only to the student of the Bible, but also to all those interested in ancient history...

Religion   **ISBN:** *1-59462-338-4*   **Pages:132**

MSRP $12.95

The Theory of Moral Sentiments
Adam Smith

QTY

This work from 1749. contains original theories of conscience amd moral judgment and it is the foundation for systemof morals.

Philosophy **ISBN:** *1-59462-777-0*   **Pages:536**

MSRP $19.95

Jessica's First Prayer
Hesba Stretton

QTY

In a screened and secluded corner of one of the many railway-bridges which span the streets of London there could be seen a few years ago, from five o'clock every morning until half past eight, a tidily set-out coffee-stall, consisting of a trestle and board, upon which stood two large tin cans, with a small fire of charcoal burning under each so as to keep the coffee boiling during the early hours of the morning when the work-people were thronging into the city on their way to their daily toil...

Pages:84

Childrens   **ISBN:** *1-59462-373-2*   *MSRP $9.95*

My Life and Work
Henry Ford

QTY

Henry Ford revolutionized the world with his implementation of mass production for the Model T automobile. Gain valuable business insight into his life and work with his own auto-biography... "We have only started on our development of our country we have not as yet, with all our talk of wonderful progress, done more than scratch the surface. The progress has been wonderful enough but..."

Pages:300

Biographies/   **ISBN:** *1-59462-198-5*   *MSRP $21.95*

The Art of Cross-Examination
Francis Wellman

I presume it is the experience of every author, after his first book is published upon an important subject, to be almost overwhelmed with a wealth of ideas and illustrations which could readily have been included in his book, and which to his own mind, at least, seem to make a second edition inevitable. Such certainly was the case with me; and when the first edition had reached its sixth impression in five months, I rejoiced to learn that it seemed to my publishers that the book had met with a sufficiently favorable reception to justify a second and considerably enlarged edition. ..

QTY

Pages:412

Reference   **ISBN: *1-59462-647-2***   *MSRP $19.95*

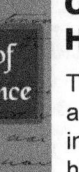

On the Duty of Civil Disobedience
Henry David Thoreau

Thoreau wrote his famous essay, On the Duty of Civil Disobedience, as a protest against an unjust but popular war and the immoral but popular institution of slave-owning. He did more than write—he declined to pay his taxes, and was hauled off to gaol in consequence. Who can say how much this refusal of his hastened the end of the war and of slavery ?

QTY

Pages:48

Law   **ISBN: *1-59462-747-9***   *MSRP $7.45*

Dream Psychology Psychoanalysis for Beginners
Sigmund Freud

Sigmund Freud, born Sigismund Schlomo Freud (May 6, 1856 - September 23, 1939), was a Jewish-Austrian neurologist and psychiatrist who co-founded the psychoanalytic school of psychology. Freud is best known for his theories of the unconscious mind, especially involving the mechanism of repression; his redefinition of sexual desire as mobile and directed towards a wide variety of objects; and his therapeutic techniques, especially his understanding of transference in the therapeutic relationship and the presumed value of dreams as sources of insight into unconscious desires.

QTY

Pages:196

Psychology   **ISBN: *1-59462-905-6***   *MSRP $15.45*

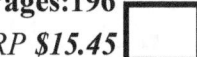

The Miracle of Right Thought
Orison Swett Marden

Believe with all of your heart that you will do what you were made to do. When the mind has once formed the habit of holding cheerful, happy, prosperous pictures, it will not be easy to form the opposite habit. It does not matter how improbable or how far away this realization may see, or how dark the prospects may be, if we visualize them as best we can, as vividly as possible, hold tenaciously to them and vigorously struggle to attain them, they will gradually become actualized, realized in the life. But a desire, a longing without endeavor, a yearning abandoned or held indifferently will vanish without realization.

QTY

Pages:360

Self Help   **ISBN: *1-59462-644-8***   *MSRP $25.45*

The Rosicrucian Cosmo-Conception Mystic Christianity by *Max Heindel*   ISBN: *1-59462-188-8*   **$38.95**
The Rosicrucian Cosmo-conception is not dogmatic, neither does it appeal to any other authority than the reason of the student. It is: not controversial, but is: sent forth in the, hope that it may help to clear...   New Age/Religion Pages 646

Abandonment To Divine Providence by *Jean-Pierre de Caussade*   ISBN: *1-59462-228-0*   **$25.95**
"The Rev. Jean Pierre de Caussade was one of the most remarkable spiritual writers of the Society of Jesus in France in the 18th Century. His death took place at Toulouse in 1751. His works have gone through many editions and have been republished...   Inspirational/Religion Pages 400

Mental Chemistry by *Charles Haanel*   ISBN: *1-59462-192-6*   **$23.95**
Mental Chemistry allows the change of material conditions by combining and appropriately utilizing the power of the mind. Much like applied chemistry creates something new and unique out of careful combinations of chemicals the mastery of mental chemistry...   New Age Pages 354

The Letters of Robert Browning and Elizabeth Barret Barrett 1845-1846 vol II   ISBN: *1-59462-193-4*   **$35.95**
by *Robert Browning* and *Elizabeth Barrett*   Biographies Pages 596

Gleanings In Genesis (volume I) by *Arthur W. Pink*   ISBN: *1-59462-130-6*   **$27.45**
Appropriately has Genesis been termed "the seed plot of the Bible" for in it we have, in germ form, almost all of the great doctrines which are afterwards fully developed in the books of Scripture which follow...   Religion/Inspirational Pages 420

The Master Key by *L. W. de Laurence*   ISBN: *1-59462-001-6*   **$30.95**
In no branch of human knowledge has there been a more lively increase of the spirit of research during the past few years than in the study of Psychology, Concentration and Mental Discipline. The requests for authentic lessons in Thought Control, Mental Discipline and...   New Age/Business Pages 422

The Lesser Key Of Solomon Goetia by *L. W. de Laurence*   ISBN: *1-59462-092-X*   **$9.95**
This translation of the first book of the "Lernegton" which is now for the first time made accessible to students of Talismanic Magic was done, after careful collation and edition, from numerous Ancient Manuscripts in Hebrew, Latin, and French...   New Age/Occult Pages 92

Rubaiyat Of Omar Khayyam by *Edward Fitzgerald*   ISBN:*1-59462-332-5*   **$13.95**
Edward Fitzgerald, whom the world has already learned, in spite of his own efforts to remain within the shadow of anonymity, to look upon as one of the rarest poets of the century, was born at Bredfield, in Suffolk, on the 31st of March, 1809. He was the third son of John Purcell...   Music Pages 172

Ancient Law by *Henry Maine*   ISBN: *1-59462-128-4*   **$29.95**
The chief object of the following pages is to indicate some of the earliest ideas of mankind, as they are reflected in Ancient Law, and to point out the relation of those ideas to modern thought.   Religion/History Pages 452

Far-Away Stories by *William J. Locke*   ISBN: *1-59462-129-2*   **$19.45**
"Good wine needs no bush,' but a collection of mixed vintages does. And this book is just such a collection. Some of the stories I do not want to remain buried for ever in the museum files of dead magazine-numbers an author's not unpardonable vanity..."   Fiction Pages 272

Life of David Crockett by *David Crockett*   ISBN: *1-59462-250-7*   **$27.45**
"Colonel David Crockett was one of the most remarkable men of the times in which he lived. Born in humble life, but gifted with a strong will, an indomitable courage, and unremitting perseverance...   Biographies/New Age Pages 424

Lip-Reading by *Edward Nitchie*   ISBN: *1-59462-206-X*   **$25.95**
Edward B. Nitchie, founder of the New York School for the Hard of Hearing, now the Nitchie School of Lip-Reading, Inc, wrote "LIP-READING Principles and Practice". The development and perfecting of this meritorious work on lip-reading was an undertaking...   How-to Pages 400

A Handbook of Suggestive Therapeutics, Applied Hypnotism, Psychic Science   ISBN: *1-59462-214-0*   **$24.95**
by *Henry Munro*   Health/New Age/Health/Self-help Pages 376

A Doll's House: and Two Other Plays by *Henrik Ibsen*   ISBN: *1-59462-112-8*   **$19.95**
Henrik Ibsen created this classic when in revolutionary 1848 Rome. Introducing some striking concepts in playwriting for the realist genre, this play has been studied the world over.   Fiction/Classics/Plays 308

The Light of Asia by *sir Edwin Arnold*   ISBN: *1-59462-204-3*   **$13.95**
In this poetic masterpiece, Edwin Arnold describes the life and teachings of Buddha. The man who was to become known as Buddha to the world was born as Prince Gautama of India but he rejected the worldly riches and abandoned the reigns of power when...   Religion/History/Biographies Pages 170

The Complete Works of Guy de Maupassant by *Guy de Maupassant*   ISBN: *1-59462-157-8*   **$16.95**
"For days and days, nights and nights, I had dreamed of that first kiss which was to consecrate our engagement, and I knew not on what spot I should put my lips..."   Fiction/Classics Pages 240

The Art of Cross-Examination by *Francis L. Wellman*   ISBN: *1-59462-309-0*   **$26.95**
Written by a renowned trial lawyer, Wellman imparts his experience and uses case studies to explain how to use psychology to extract desired information through questioning.   How-to/Science/Reference Pages 408

Answered or Unanswered? by *Louisa Vaughan*   ISBN: *1-59462-248-5*   **$10.95**
Miracles of Faith in China   Religion Pages 112

The Edinburgh Lectures on Mental Science (1909) by *Thomas*   ISBN: *1-59462-008-3*   **$11.95**
This book contains the substance of a course of lectures recently given by the writer in the Queen Street Hall, Edinburgh. Its purpose is to indicate the Natural Principles governing the relation between Mental Action and Material Conditions...   New Age/Psychology Pages 148

Ayesha by *H. Rider Haggard*   ISBN: *1-59462-301-5*   **$24.95**
Verily and indeed it is the unexpected that happens! Probably if there was one person upon the earth from whom the Editor of this, and of a certain previous history, did not expect to hear again...   Classics Pages 380

Ayala's Angel by *Anthony Trollope*   ISBN: *1-59462-352-X*   **$29.95**
The two girls were both pretty, but Lucy who was twenty-one who supposed to be simple and comparatively unattractive, whereas Ayala was credited, as her Bombwhat romantic name might show, with poetic charm and a taste for romance. Ayala when her father died was nineteen...   Fiction Pages 484

The American Commonwealth by *James Bryce*   ISBN: *1-59462-286-8*   **$34.45**
An interpretation of American democratic political theory. It examines political mechanics and society from the perspective of Scotsman James Bryce   Politics Pages 572

Stories of the Pilgrims by *Margaret P. Pumphrey*   ISBN: *1-59462-116-0*   **$17.95**
This book explores pilgrims religious oppression in England as well as their escape to Holland and eventual crossing to America on the Mayflower, and their early days in New England...   History Pages 268

QTY

The Fasting Cure *by Sinclair Upton*　　　　　　　　　　　　ISBN: *1-59462-222-1*　**$13.95**
In the Cosmopolitan Magazine for May, 1910, and in the Contemporary Review (London) for April, 1910, I published an article dealing with my experiences in fasting. I have written a great many magazine articles, but never one which attracted so much attention... New Age/Self Help/Health Pages 164

Hebrew Astrology *by Sepharial*　　　　　　　　　　　　　ISBN: *1-59462-308-2*　**$13.45**
In these days of advanced thinking it is a matter of common observation that we have left many of the old landmarks behind and that we are now pressing forward to greater heights and to a wider horizon than that which represented the mind-content of our progenitors... Astrology Pages 144

Thought Vibration or The Law of Attraction in the Thought World　　ISBN: *1-59462-127-6*　**$12.95**
by William Walker Atkinson　　　　　　　　　　　　　　　　Psychology/Religion Pages 144

Optimism *by Helen Keller*　　　　　　　　　　　　　　　ISBN: *1-59462-108-X*　**$15.95**
Helen Keller was blind, deaf, and mute since 19 months old, yet famously learned how to overcome these handicaps, communicate with the world, and spread her lectures promoting optimism. An inspiring read for everyone... Biographies/Inspirational Pages 84

Sara Crewe *by Frances Burnett*　　　　　　　　　　　　　ISBN: *1-59462-360-0*　**$9.45**
In the first place, Miss Minchin lived in London. Her home was a large, dull, tall one, in a large, dull square, where all the houses were alike, and all the sparrows were alike, and where all the door-knockers made the same heavy sound... Childrens/Classic Pages 88

The Autobiography of Benjamin Franklin *by Benjamin Franklin*　　ISBN: *1-59462-135-7*　**$24.95**
The Autobiography of Benjamin Franklin has probably been more extensively read than any other American historical work, and no other book of its kind has had such ups and downs of fortune. Franklin lived for many years in England, where he was agent... Biographies/History Pages 332

Name	
Email	
Telephone	
Address	
City, State ZIP	

☐ **Credit Card**　　　　　　☐ **Check / Money Order**

Credit Card Number	
Expiration Date	
Signature	

Please Mail to:　Book Jungle
PO Box 2226
Champaign, IL 61825
or Fax to:　　　630-214-0564

ORDERING INFORMATION

web: *www.bookjungle.com*
email: *sales@bookjungle.com*
fax: *630-214-0564*
mail: *Book Jungle PO Box 2226 Champaign, IL 61825*
or PayPal *to sales@bookjungle.com*

Please contact us for bulk discounts

DIRECT-ORDER TERMS

**20% Discount if You Order
Two or More Books**
Free Domestic Shipping!
Accepted: Master Card, Visa,
Discover, American Express